W9-CSR-426

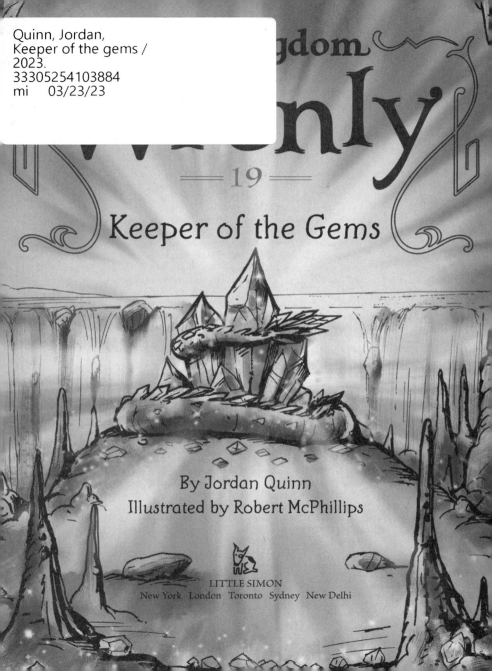

gdom

nly

— 19 —

Keeper of the Gems

By Jordan Quinn

Illustrated by Robert McPhillips

LITTLE SIMON

New York London Toronto Sydney New Delhi

LITTLE SIMON

An imprint of Simon & Schuster Children's Publishing Division
1230 Avenue of the Americas, New York, New York 10020
First Little Simon hardcover edition February 2023
Also available in a Little Simon paperback edition.
Copyright © 2023 by Simon & Schuster, Inc.
All rights reserved, including the right of reproduction in whole or in part in any form.
LITTLE SIMON is a registered trademark of Simon & Schuster, Inc., and associated colophon is a trademark of Simon & Schuster, Inc.
For information about special discounts for bulk purchases, please contact Simon & Schuster Special Sales at 1-866-506-1949 or business@simonandschuster.com.
The Simon & Schuster Speakers Bureau can bring authors to your live event. For more information or to book an event contact the Simon & Schuster Speakers Bureau at 1-866-248-3049 or visit our website at www.simonspeakers.com.
Manufactured in the United States of America 0123 LAK
2 4 6 8 10 9 7 5 3 1
Library of Congress Cataloging-in-Publication Data
Names: Quinn, Jordan, author. | McPhillips, Robert, 1971– illustrator.
Title: Keeper of the gems / by Jordan Quinn ; illustrated by Robert McPhillips.
Description: First Little Simon edition. | New York : Little Simon, 2023. | Series: The Kingdom of Wrenly ; 19 | Audience: Ages 5–9. | Summary: The gnomes of the Stone Forest are in trouble when all the gems in the forest lose their shine, so Prince Lucas and Lady Clara help the gnomes before their home changes forever.
Identifiers: LCCN 2022042804 (print) | LCCN 2022042805 (ebook) | ISBN 9781665919319 (paperback) | ISBN 9781665919326 (hardcover) | ISBN 9781665919333 (ebook)
Subjects: CYAC: Gnomes—Fiction. | Gems—Fiction. | Magic—Fiction. | LCGFT: Novels.
Classification: LCC PZ7.Q31945 Ke 2023 (print) | LCC PZ7.Q31945 (ebook) | DDC [Fic]—dc23
LC record available at https://lccn.loc.gov/2022042804
LC ebook record available at https://lccn.loc.gov/2022042805

CONTENTS

CHAPTER 1

The Glitter End

The most beautiful jewels in the kingdom of Wrenly came from deep within the caverns that lie beneath the Stone Forest.

The gnomes of Wrenly mined the gems, like diamonds and pearls, for the kingdom.

Pilwinkle, the chief of the gnomes, was in charge of everything that went on in the Stone Forest.

He was especially proud to oversee the building of a new fountain in the center of the Den of Diamonds. When it was done, water would spout from the top and spill over the edges until it reached the bottom.

The gnomes chiseled away at the fountain.

With all this work going on, it was extra noisy in the caverns. But the gnomes loved the sound of hard work.

As Pilwinkle made his rounds, a gnome named Wayrich tapped him urgently on the arm.

"Chief Pilwinkle!" cried Wayrich. "Something's amiss in the Pearly Gates!"

The Pearly Gates was a cavern filled with big shells that grew freshwater pearls. It was right next to the Den of Diamonds, so Pilwinkle followed his worried friend to see what was happening.

Once there, Wayrich pried open a shell and held it in front of Pilwinkle. The chief gnome inspected the pearl inside. Instead of finding a shiny white pearl with a rainbow of colors, he saw nothing but a dull white stone.

"Well, what is one dud among so many?" said Pilwinkle.

Wayrich shook his head. "But it's not *one* dud! It's happening to *all* of our freshwater pearls."

Pilwinkle asked to see more pearls. The more he saw, the more fearful he became.

"Oh my. Pearls without shine are *worthless!*" he shouted.

The gnomes stopped working when they heard Pilwinkle's cry. They began to murmur to one another about the lifeless pearls.

Dalfoodle, another gnome, rushed to Pilwinkle's side. "The same thing is happening in the Den of Diamonds!" he exclaimed. "The diamonds are losing their sparkle, and we've even spied cracks in the cavern walls too."

Pilwinkle tugged his long white beard. "This is deeply troubling," he said as he followed Dalfoodle back to the Den of Diamonds.

Dalfoodle showed Pilwinkle a rough-cut diamond. It had no sparkle. When Pilwinkle saw the cracks in the cavern walls, his eyes grew wide.

"What is going on?" he cried. "I've worked in the Stone Forest caverns my whole life, and I've never seen anything like this!"

Pilwinkle knew what he had to do. It was something he had never done before: ask the king for help.

CHAPTER 2

Mission Gem-Possible

BOOM!

BOOM!

A palace cannon fired.

Prince Lucas pulled back the reins on his horse, Ivan.

Clara did the same with her horse, Scallop.

Two cannon fires meant the kids had to return to the palace *at once*.

"Let's go!" said the prince.

The kids turned their horses around and galloped back to the stable. Then they raced up the stone stairs to the palace and ran all the way to the king's great hall.

King Caleb sat on his throne. On one side of him stood Grom—one of Wrenly's top wizards—and on the other side stood Sir Desdan, the kingdom's bravest knight.

What's Grom doing here? the prince wondered.

Grom had canceled potions class earlier in the day, which was why the kids had been out riding. Sir Desdan's presence beside the king was also unusual.

"You called, Father?" asked the prince.

King Caleb folded his arms and said, "Yes. We've received an odd message from Pilwinkle, chief of the gnomes. There's an emergency in the Stone Forest caverns."

Lucas and Clara looked at each other and then back at the king.

"It seems the beautiful jewels within the caverns are turning into worthless rocks," the king went on. "The trouble is spreading throughout the caverns, and to make matters worse, the cavern walls are cracking."

"Cracking?" Clara asked. "That's bad."

"It is," agreed the king. "Now, Grom has samples from the caverns to study in his lab. Meanwhile, Sir Desdan has led the gnomes out of the caverns to safety."

Lucas stepped forward. "Father, are the caves in danger?"

King Caleb nodded. "The cracks in the walls are deepening, and more cracks are forming," said the king. "The caverns could indeed collapse."

"How may we help, Your Majesty?" Clara asked.

The king looked gravely at both children. "You two have solved some of the kingdom's most difficult mysteries. Would you be willing to work with Pilwinkle to help solve the mystery of the dying jewels?"

"Absolutely," said the prince.

"We would be honored," Clara added.

The children both bowed before King Caleb as he wished them well.

Then Lucas and Clara raced to get Ruskin, the prince's scarlet dragon. Time was running out . . . and Ruskin would get them to the Stone Forest faster than the horses.

23

CHAPTER 3

Dragon Fear

Ruskin circled above the Stone Forest while Lucas and Clara sat in a special gondola. The prince had built it for the dragon to carry.

The pillars and towers below teemed with gnomes who had left the caverns.

Lucas spied Pilwinkle standing by a cave entrance and asked Ruskin to land.

As the dragon got closer the gnomes scattered to hide. Ruskin touched down and folded his wings to his sides.

The kids leaped from the gondola and called to Pilwinkle.

"Welcome, Prince Lucas and Lady Clara!" said Pilwinkle. "And, Ruskin, my, how you've grown since we last saw you!"

The dragon nodded.

Lucas noticed the other gnomes peeking out from behind stones and rocks. It was as if they wanted to stay far away from the young dragon.

Lucas realized how fearsome Ruskin might look to the gnomes. It's not every day that a dragon flew over and landed in one's village.

The young prince turned to the frightened crowd and said, "No need to worry. This is Ruskin. He is friendly and kind to all."

Ruskin sat down on all fours and bowed his head gently to the gnomes.

"We've been told you're having trouble in the caverns," Lucas said, "and we've come to help."

Pilwinkle, along with Wayrich, Dalfoodle, and Lumbiddle, stepped closer.

"It's terribly upsetting," Pilwinkle said. "The gems and the caverns seem to be dying—and quickly."

"Our gems have lost their sparkle!" said Wayrich.

"And it's getting worse by the moment!" Dalfoodle added.

Pilwinkle put a finger to his lips and hushed the others. "Enough! Remember, we must not upset our fellow gnomes any further."

Then the chief gnome waved Lucas and Clara toward the entrance to one of the caves.

Inside the cave Pilwinkle handed torches to Lucas and Clara. Then the four gnomes led the way into the caverns while Ruskin stood guard at the entrance.

The kids studied the jagged crystals that hung from the ceilings and the gems along the walls.

None of them shimmered. Everything looked gray and dark, like any ordinary cave.

Clara could even see cracks forming in the walls.

"Can you think of *anything* that might be causing these problems?" she asked. "Any changes in your mining routines?"

"None," said Pilwinkle. "Until yesterday, we've been mining and collecting gems as usual. We *are* building a new fountain, though. It's been noisy and messy, but that is normal. Come see."

Pilwinkle led the kids to the fountain in the Den of Diamonds.

"We built this fountain to honor the beauty and purity of the gems within our caverns," he said with a sigh. "If our caverns go to ruin, what will become of the gnomes?"

"Don't worry," said the prince. "We'll solve this mystery together."

Clara crouched by an old plaque leaning against the base of the fountain. The tablet looked much older than the rest of the stone used for the fountain. It was also broken in several places, with pieces missing like an unfinished puzzle.

"This is curious," Clara said. She wiped the dust from the tablet, and words appeared. "It says, 'Bezel, the Keeper of the Gems.'"

Lucas looked at Pilwinkle and asked, "Bezel? Who's Bezel?"

CHAPTER 4

Bezel,
the Keeper
of the Gems

The Legend of Bezel

Pilwinkle took a deep breath and began his story.

"Bezel is thought to be a magical creature living deep within the walls of these caverns. As the legend goes, Bezel is supposed to be the Keeper of the Gems as well as the protector of the caverns."

Lucas held his torch in front of the plaque.

"Is there any *truth* to this legend?" he asked.

"We've never actually *seen* the Keeper. Bezel is just a wonderful part of our gnome folklore," Pilwinkle said. "Now, this . . . We found the tablet in pieces while digging on the very spot where the fountain now sits. We were planning to put it back together and make it part of the fountain to honor the legend of Bezel."

Pilwinkle tipped the tablet forward and pulled out another

broken piece that lay behind it. "We're still working on it, as you can see."

Clara looked at the new piece. It had only one word: "must."

"Hmm, that piece fits here," she said. Then she read the new sentence aloud. "The Keeper of the Gems must."

"The Keeper of the Gems must *what*?" asked Lucas.

Bezel, the Keeper of the Gems, must

Pilwinkle shrugged. "Without the other missing pieces, we're not sure," he explained. "But *we* must save the caverns. That is more important than any old legend."

The prince scratched his head and said, "Well, it must be a powerful legend to have a message carved into a tablet that was hidden deep within the caverns."

Pilwinkle and the three gnomes nodded. "It is powerful," said Pilwinkle. "The legend has always brought us comfort and made gnomes feel safe—that is, until now."

He sighed and beckoned everyone to follow. "Let's keep moving. There's much more to see, and we may be running out of time."

Pilwinkle showed them the Emerald Oasis, which looked like nothing more than a dark pool of water surrounded by craggy black walls.

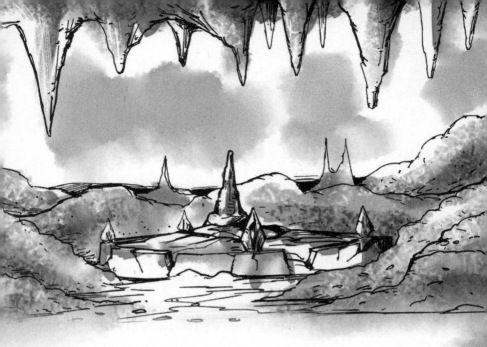

The Fountain of Sapphires looked
like a gravel pit, and the River of
Rubies ran muddy brown.

"This is more dire than I
imagined," said the prince. "What
could have destroyed the gems so
quickly?"

Before anyone could answer, a loud crack came from the ceiling above them.

"Oh, boulders!" cried Pilwinkle. "We must leave the caverns at once! I fear it's no longer safe."

Everyone raced down the tunnel as *another* sound echoed from the rock walls. Only it was not a crack this time. It was a long, howling wail.

Pilwinkle stopped and whispered, "What was *that*?!"

Another howl erupted and trailed off. Now the sound was even closer. Lucas, Clara, and the gnomes stood still in the silence . . . waiting for another howl. Then, without warning, the cavern floor began to rumble and shake.

The gnomes and kids held out their arms to keep from falling.

SQUAWK! screeched Ruskin, who had sensed danger and flew in to help. He landed in the trembling tunnel.

"Thanks, Ruskin!" Lucas cried.

The prince scrambled into the gondola, then pulled the others in one by one. Once they were all aboard, Ruskin took off, dodging the falling rocks and escaping through the caverns.

Lucas heard another howl over the rumbling. *It almost sounds like something is trapped in the cavern walls,* he thought. *But that's impossible . . . right?*

CHAPTER 5

Great Balls of Fire!

Rocks tumbled from the top and sides of the cavern around them. Ruskin veered one way and then another. *Whoosh!* He rocketed everyone to safety. They watched as boulders filled the mouth of the cave. The entrance had been completely sealed shut.

"That was close!" Clara cried. "We could've been trapped in there!"

"You saved us, Ruskin!" said the prince, patting his dragon.

Ruskin landed, and everyone climbed out of the gondola. The gnomes even kissed the ground, happy to be back on solid land.

"No more flying for us," said Pilwinkle. "A gnome's home is *in* or *under* the Stone Forest."

"Exactly!" Wayrich cried. "So *now* what do we do? Gnomes without the caverns are gnomes without a home!"

Pilwinkle wiped the sweat from his brow. "Well, first let's be glad we're all safe. But Wayrich makes a good point. We'll have to get back inside in order to solve this mystery."

Lucas walked toward the boulders blocking the entrance. "Let's fly to the other entrance and see if we can get in that way," he said.

"Are you sure you don't want to walk?" Pilwinkle asked, but he knew that they must move fast.

Ruskin waited for his passengers
to climb back on board. Then he
lifted into the air and flew to the
other side of the cavern. But this
entrance was blocked by boulders
too.

"We're too late," said Clara. "Is there another way in?"

Pilwinkle pulled out his pickax. "We could dig our way through!"

The prince shook his head. "That will take too long."

Dalfoodle pointed to the wall of tumbled boulders. "There's a space at the top of the fallen rocks," he said. "We could squeeze through there!"

Pilwinkle folded his arms. "I'd rather dig."

Then Ruskin let out a screech that got everyone's attention. The scarlet dragon flew toward the entrance and opened his mouth.

"Hold on, everyone!" cried the prince. Ruskin has a scorching idea that might fire you up!"

The gnomes ducked down into the gondola as Ruskin gulped in a huge breath of air and blew a long stream of fire at the boulders.

The rocks exploded from the cave's opening, and a new entrance was formed.

The crew hopped back onto the
ground as Pilwinkle lit emergency
torches using the flames from
Ruskin's blast.

"I'm glad you're on our side," Pilwinkle told Ruskin.

"What now?" asked Dalfoodle.

"Simple," said Clara. "We enter the dark caverns, find out what's making that creepy howling, and bring back the shimmer, shine, and hope to the Stone Forest. Who's with me?"

The crew looked at one another
and held their torches aloft.
"Onward!" they cried.

CHAPTER 6

Something's *There*!

Pilwinkle led the group through the caverns to look for clues. The walls looked bleaker and more cheerless than ever—not the tiniest bit of sparkle remained.

When they reached the mouth of the tunnel that led to the River of Rubies, it was filled with gravel and rocks.

"Dead end," said Lucas.

"The earthquake blocked this entrance too," Pilwinkle said, "but it's mostly loose rocks, so we'll be able to clear it."

The gnomes pulled out their pickaxes, which they always carried with them.

"We'll do whatever it takes!" said Wayrich.

"That's right!" said Lumbiddle. "This rubble is no match for us!"

The prince was happy to see that the gnomes had lost their fear and were ready to save the caverns.

Everyone propped their torches between the rocks and got to work.

Tink! Tink! Tink! The gnomes pecked at the rocks and rubble with their pickaxes. Lucas and Clara shoveled the rubble to one side. Ruskin stood guard.

Suddenly the dragon perked his wings up and crept away from the group. He began to growl, and then he squawked sharply.

Everyone stopped working to marvel at what had gotten the dragon's attention. And what they saw took their breath away.

A strange beast stood in the middle of the tunnel. It was long like a dragon, but with scales made of jewels that glowed bright against the darkness of the cavern walls. The creature's eyes were big, bright, and bold . . . and they were staring directly back at the crew.

Without warning, the creature lowered its head as if it was going to attack.

Ruskin screeched and flapped forward.

"Wait! Stop!" Pilwinkle shouted, running in front of the dragon and waving his arms.

Ruskin stepped back and exhaled without releasing any fire. The beast began to run toward them.

"Look out!" the prince cried.

Everyone pressed themselves tight against the sides of the cavern. The beast raced by them and scurried through a thin crack in the fallen rubble.

Pilwinkle was the first to pull himself away from the wall.

"Did we find Bezel?" he wondered out loud. "The Keeper of the Gems?"

CHAPTER 7

Puzzle Piece

"It must be Bezel!" Pilwinkle said.

The gnomes' eyes grew wide with joy as they threw their arms around one another.

"To think Bezel has been living inside the cavern all along," Pilwinkle cheered. "And now our protector has come to help!"

The prince placed his hand on Pilwinkle's shoulder.

"I'm afraid this may be good news *and* bad news," said Lucas. "The good news is, the legend is true, but the bad news is, Bezel is no longer protecting the gnomes or the caverns."

Clara nodded. "We still need to solve this mystery."

"I wonder if Bezel has the answer we're seeking," said Pilwinkle as he grabbed his pickax. "We shall clear the rest of this rubble and follow the Keeper!"

The excitement of seeing Bezel made the crew work even faster than before.

They loosened the rocks and threw them to the side. Clara was about to hurl a flat piece of stone when she noticed something unusual.

"Look what I found!" she cried, brushing the dirt from the stone. "This has writing on it like the other tablet!"

Pilwinkle and the other gnomes stopped digging.

"What does it say?" Pilwinkle asked.

Clara carefully blew off the dust to reveal a new word. "It says . . . 'peace.'"

Pilwinkle gasped. "I've seen this type of stone before. It *is* the same stone used for the tablet by the new fountain!"

"That one said 'The Keeper of the Gems must,' but then the words stopped because the stone was broken," Clara remembered.

"Aha!" cried Lucas. "Now, *this* is a clue! Everyone look for more flat rocks shaped like this one."

The crew searched through the rubble and found more flat stones. They set them on the ground next to one another, but the words were jumbled.

Finally, Pilwinkle cracked the code.

"I've got it!" he announced. "The message says, 'The Keeper of the Gems must . . . always . . . be . . . at . . . *PEACE!*'"

"Hooray!" shouted the gnomes, and they began to dance in a circle.

"Hold up, friends!" the prince said. "As wonderful as this discovery is, we still have a problem. Bezel should be at *peace*, and right now the Keeper does *not* look at peace!"

"The prince is right," Pilwinkle said. "We must find Bezel and help."

Lucas nodded and wondered aloud, "What could have bothered Bezel in the first place?"

Clara looked at the broken pieces of tablet. "Maybe it has something to do with these," she suggested.

"My goodness, you are right," the chief gnome said. "It was the construction of the fountain. We must have disturbed Bezel's peace!"

Clara collected the tablet pieces and handed them to Pilwinkle.

"Here," she said. "Keep these until we get back to the fountain. Perhaps we can still make things right if these pieces are the key."

CHAPTER 8

Trust Me

The gnomes chipped away at the rocks with their pickaxes until they broke through to the other side, where Bezel had gone.

The prince held his torch in the opening.

"All clear on the other side," he said. "Let's go!"

They grabbed their torches and, one by one, climbed through the hole.

"Look!" cried Clara, pointing. "I see Bezel!"

The Keeper stood silently in the tunnel. It was almost as if he was waiting for them.

"What do we do now?" Dalfoodle whispered.

Pilwinkle put a finger to his lips. "Let's be quiet," he said. "We don't want to scare Bezel away this time."

The prince went to Pilwinkle and whispered, "I have an idea."

Pilwinkle turned an ear toward the prince. "What is it?"

"We have to earn Bezel's trust," said the prince.

The most important thing Lucas and Clara had learned with magical creatures was: You have to win their trust.

"Bezel is afraid of us," the prince went on. "Just like the gnomes were afraid when they first saw Ruskin."

"That's right," Pilwinkle said. "Once you showed us Ruskin was trustworthy, we were no longer afraid of him."

"Exactly," the prince said.

"Well, I guess it's time for us to put our special skills to the test," Clara said with a smile. "Let's make an ally out of an enemy."

CHAPTER 9

Take a Bow

"First we need to show Bezel that our dragon means no harm," Lucas whispered to the gnomes. "When Ruskin tried to protect us earlier, he must have scared Bezel."

The prince waved toward the dragon and gave a hand signal. Ruskin nodded and sat down. Everyone watched to see what Ruskin would do next, including Bezel.

Now it was Clara's turn. She slowly bowed before the dragon. This showed her respect for Ruskin.

Ruskin bowed back to show his respect for Clara.

"Good boy," Clara whispered and patted him gently.

The gnomes were impressed by the way Ruskin and Clara had shown their trust in each other. Bezel noticed it too.

Now it was time to win over Bezel's trust. Pilwinkle stepped closer to Bezel, but not so close as to alarm the magical beast.

The gnome made eye contact with Bezel. Then he slowly bowed before the Keeper and held up a gem he had stashed in his pocket.

Bezel, in turn, bowed back to Pilwinkle. Now the others needed to do the same thing.

As soon as they bowed, a sense of calm filled the cavern. The air felt lighter as Bezel's glowing body relaxed. The trust had been achieved!

Lucas held his breath, hoping that Bezel would let them know what to do next.

Then the magical creature did just that.

With a soft howl, Bezel seemed to say *"Follow me."* The Keeper walked farther down the tunnel.

And everyone followed.

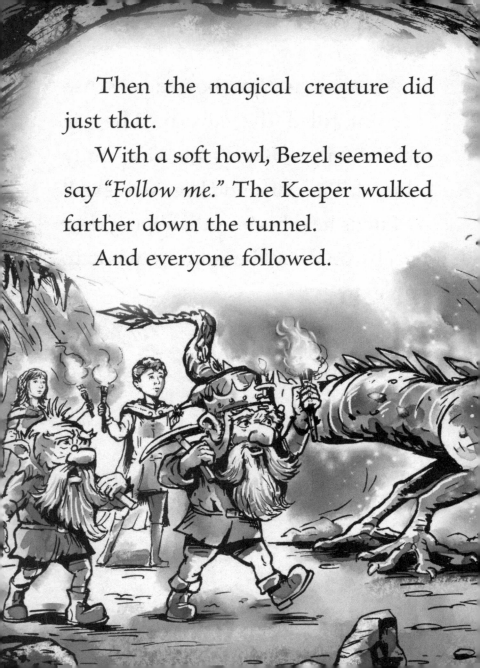

CHAPTER 10

All Aglow

Bezel led them to the Den of Diamonds and wrapped himself around the fountain. The Keeper pawed at the broken tablet and whimpered.

"The tablet," said Clara. "We need to fix the broken tablet."

Pilwinkle took the missing pieces and motioned to the fountain. Bezel nodded as if to say *"Yes!"*

The chief gnome went to work, attaching the missing pieces and locking them back into place.

All at once Bezel and the fountain began to glow until a warm light burst from the fountain's spout and swirled to the top of the cavern. Brightness washed over the rock walls and flowed down the tunnels. The caverns were coming back to life—even the cracks in the walls began to fill in.

The gnomes squealed with delight as they watched the sparkle and shine return.

Bezel,
the Keeper
of the Gems
must always
be at peace.

Suddenly water bubbled naturally from the fountain's top and spilled into the basin below. And with the water, a rock door creaked open.

"Look! An entrance is forming at the base of the fountain!" cried Pilwinkle.

"That must be Bezel's home!" Clara cried. "The Keeper of the Gems lives beneath the fountain!"

"And now the Keeper is at peace," said Pilwinkle.

Bezel,
the Keeper
of the Gems
must always
be at peace.

Bezel bowed again to say thank you to the gnomes, who bowed their heads back. The time had come for the Keeper of the Gems to return to its peaceful state. Bezel glided with the water through the open door . . . finally back home.

A new sound rang out as the door shut behind Bezel. It was a sound of hope, happiness, and peace that Lucas and Clara would never forget.

Pilwinkle spun in a circle. "Our beautiful Stone Forest caverns have been *saved!*"

The kids and the gnomes held hands and danced in a circle around the fountain.

"To thank you for your help, we have a gnome tradition," Pilwinkle told Lucas and Clara. "Wait here, please."

Pilwinkle and the gnomes ran off to get something. Lucas and Clara sat and admired the beauty of the fountain and the twinkling gems around them.

When the gnomes returned, Pilwinkle held out three diamond-and-sapphire pendants—one for Lucas, one for Clara, and one for Ruskin.

"We call these forever necklaces," Pilwinkle said. "According to our legends, these necklaces carry the peace and protection of Bezel for all the days of your lives."

Lucas and Clara examined the necklaces, while Ruskin sniffed at his.

"They're beautiful," said the prince. "Thank you, Pilwinkle, Chief of the Gnomes."

"We are so honored," Clara added.

Pilwinkle smiled. "I know that Bezel is smiling up at you from below," he said. "The Keeper will keep you safe."

The crew made their way back through the caverns to the entrance where all the rubble had magically been removed.

When they exited the cave, Pilwinkle let out a joyful howl.

"Attention, fellow gnomes! Our caverns have been restored!" he shouted to the crowd waiting outside. "It's now safe to go back inside and continue our humble work!"

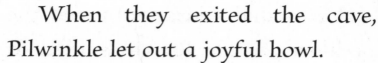

The gnomes cheered and clapped.
All was right in the Stone Forest
again.

Lucas and Clara smiled at the happy villagers. If they thought the gnomes were excited now, wait until Pilwinkle shared the news that the legend of the Keeper of the Gems was true.